THIS WALKER BOOK BELONGS TO:

_____

_____

_____

_____

For Hannah and Zoe,
a couple of first-rate schoolgirls
A. H.

For Alex and Bump
J. B.

First published 1999 by Walker Books Ltd
87 Vauxhall Walk, London SE11 5HJ

This edition published 2000

2 4 6 8 10 9 7 5 3 1

Text © 1999 Amy Hest
Illustrations © 1999 Jill Barton

This book has been typeset in Opti Lucius.

Printed in Hong Kong

British Library Cataloguing in Publication Data
A catalogue record for this book is
available from the British Library.

ISBN 0-7445-7776-4

Off to School, Baby Duck!

by **Amy Hest**

illustrated by **Jill Barton**

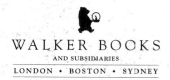

WALKER BOOKS
AND SUBSIDIARIES
LONDON • BOSTON • SYDNEY

Baby Duck could not eat her breakfast.
It was the first day of school,
and her stomach was all jitters!
"Breakfast toast is very tasty," said Mrs Duck.
"Won't you have a bite?"
"No," Baby said.
"Breakfast juice is very juicy," said Mr Duck.
"Won't you have a sip?"
"No," Baby said.

"Your sister Hot Stuff is much too small
  to go to school," Mrs Duck pointed out.
"She's not brave enough, either.
  Aren't you glad you're big and brave?"
"No," Baby said.

Baby Duck sat under the table
with her blue school bag.
Baby loved her school bag,
and the important things inside:
one favourite book,
a sandwich with jam,
one tall pad
and one yellow pencil
(a special going-to-school
present from
Hot Stuff).

"Button up your new
school cardigan!"
called Mrs Duck.
"Hurry, Baby!"

Baby buttoned. It took a long time.

"Buckle up your new
school shoes!"
called Mr Duck.
"Hurry, Baby!"

Baby buckled. It took a long time.

Mr Duck looked at his watch.
"Time to go!" he cried.

Mr and Mrs Duck bustled out of the front
door, swinging Hot Stuff in the air.
Their feet crunched on dry leaves.
"Come, come!" they cried.
"School, glorious school!"
Baby Duck dragged behind.
"Goodbye, house," she whispered
in a little small voice.

The Duck family waddled down the road.
"Hop to it, Baby!" called Mr Duck.
Baby could not hop. Her feet felt too heavy.

"Chin up, Baby!" called Mrs Duck. "Skip along!"
Baby could not skip. Her school bag was
bumping. *Bumpity bumpity bump.*

The Duck family waddled through the school
gate. Baby's buckle popped open and her shoe
started flapping. *Flappity flappity flap.*

"Calling all babies! Here I am!"
Grandpa was waiting on a bench.
Baby sat up close to Grandpa.
"Rough day?" he whispered.
"Yes," Baby said.
"Long walk?" whispered Grandpa.
"Yes," Baby said.
"Scared about school?"
whispered Grandpa.
"Yes," Baby said.
"Yes, yes, yes!"

"Sometimes it helps to sing a song,"
Grandpa said. "You sing nice songs, Baby."
"Yes," Baby said. "I do." Then Baby sang a song.

"Please don't make me go to school.
My teacher will be mean.
I won't have any fun or friends.
And who will buckle my new shoe?"

"I will," Grandpa said.
And he buckled Baby's shoe.

After that Baby showed Grandpa
the important things inside her school bag.
He liked the pencil from Hot Stuff.
"You draw nice pictures, Baby,"
Grandpa pointed out.
"Yes," Baby said. "I do."

Then Baby drew a picture.

Davy Duck took little steps towards Baby.

He looked at Baby's picture.

Baby felt proud.

Miss Posy came across the playground.

"My name is Miss Posy," she said.

"I'm the teacher."

"Are you mean?" Grandpa asked.

"Oh, no!" said Miss Posy.

"Do you sing songs in
    your school?" Grandpa asked.

"Oh, yes!" said Miss Posy.

"Do you read books in there?" Grandpa asked.
"Oh, yes!" said Miss Posy.
"Do you like sandwiches with jam and yellow pencils?" Grandpa asked.
"Oh, yes!" said Miss Posy.

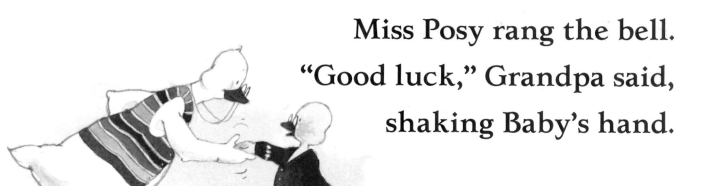

Miss Posy rang the bell.
"Good luck," Grandpa said,
shaking Baby's hand.

Then Mr and Mrs Duck
took turns kissing
Baby on both
cheeks.

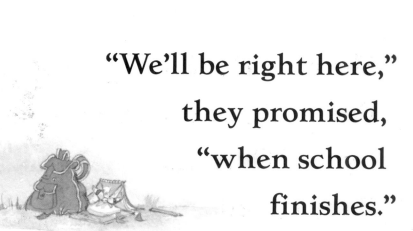

"We'll be right here,"
they promised,
"when school
finishes."

But Hot Stuff cried,
"Wa, waa,
waaaa!"

Baby Duck put her arm
round Hot Stuff.
"Little small babies have
to wait," she said.

She gave Hot Stuff
the picture she had
made. "Chin up!"
Baby called.

Then Baby Duck hopped and skipped up the steps to school with her new friend Davy Duck.

She sang a pretty song.

"Off to school, Baby Duck!
I am big and brave.
I like Miss Posy, Davy Duck too.
And I'll have fun at school!"

Off to School, Baby Duck!

AMY HEST says, "It's been a long time since I was a schoolgirl, but I STILL remember those first-day blues. Knots in my stomach and all those secret worries. Would I have a friend? Would my teacher like me? If only I could just stay home… Funny, I really liked school, maybe even loved school, once I got rid of those first-day blues."

As well as the four Baby Duck stories, Amy Hest has written many tales about children and grandparents, including her Walker titles *Rosie's Fishing Trip*, *Jamaica Louise James* and *When Jessie Came Across the Sea*. She lives in the USA.

JILL BARTON says that this story evokes strong memories. "'Goodbye house' – I remember thinking those very words when facing the great adventure of starting school. I drew a one-room schoolhouse because it seemed right; I would enjoy attending it if I were Baby Duck. Miss Posy drew herself and is based on a favourite teacher of mine, even down to her lace-up shoes."

Jill Barton has illustrated many children's books. Among them are *The Pig in the Pond*, which was Highly Commended for the Kate Greenaway Medal, *The Happy Hedgehog Band*, *Little Mo* and *What Baby Wants*. She lives in Devon.

ISBN 0-7445-5220-6 (pb)

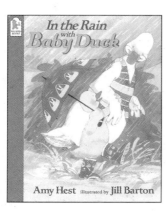

ISBN 0-7445-6323-2 (pb)

ISBN 0-7445-6305-4 (pb)

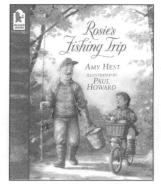

ISBN 0-7445-4703-2 (pb)